MY ADVENTURES
WITH

This book was especially written for
Madeline Worster
with love from
Mom and Dad

Adapted by Kate Andresen

ISBN 978-1-875676-48-4

As the sun rose over the horizon, Minnie threw open the window to greet the new day. The sky was blue, the birds were singing, and a cool breeze drifted through the window.

It was a special day today.

Minnie smiled. "What a perfect day to celebrate a birthday! My friends will be so happy when they receive their invitations to my surprise picnic!" she exclaimed.

Minnie made invitations for everybody, then wrote a list of all the things she would need for the picnic. She put them into her basket together with a new tablecloth, napkins and plates, and then headed out the door.

Things for Picnic:
Tablecloth
Napkins
Plates
Fruit Salad
Lemonade
Corn on the Cob
Hot Dogs
Buns
Ketchup
Mustard

Madeline Worster lived nearby in Overland Park. Today was January 15th, her birthday, and Madeline was spending the day with her friends at the Clubhouse.

She found Minnie in the garden picking flowers. Minnie greeted her friend and presented her with a beautiful bunch of carnations. "Happy birthday, Madeline!"

"Thank you, Minnie! Carnations are my birth flower," said Madeline.

"I know!" replied Minnie smiling. "Wait here, Madeline, while I take your flowers back to the Clubhouse and put them in a vase."

A moment later Daisy strolled into the garden and the two friends greeted each other warmly. Soon, Daisy noticed Minnie's basket on the lawn.

"What's this?" wondered Daisy as she opened the basket. Inside, she found an invitation addressed to her, and a shopping list.

"Oh, Minnie is planning a picnic! What fun!" thought Daisy. "I'll make a fruit salad."

"We'll see Minnie later, Madeline. Let's go and pick some blueberries," said Daisy as she picked up Minnie's basket.

"OK, I do like blueberries," replied Madeline.

Soon their bags and pockets were full and they couldn't carry any more.

"I'll go and get a bowl to hold all the blueberries. I won't be long, Madeline," said Daisy.

So off she went, leaving Madeline and Minnie's basket by the blueberry bush.

As soon as Daisy got back to the kitchen, she washed the blueberries and put them into a large bowl.

"Now, all I need is a big, juicy watermelon, and a pineapple, and it will be a delicious fruit salad!" she said.

Forgetting that she said she would go back to the blueberry bush, Daisy headed to the watermelon patch instead!

Meanwhile, when Minnie returned to the garden, she saw that Madeline and the picnic basket had gone!

"Madeline, Madeline!" called Minnie. But there was no reply from her friend. "Where could they be?" thought Minnie.

She looked everywhere, but there was no sign of them anywhere.

After a while, Minnie returned to the Clubhouse and plopped into a chair.

"Oh, no!" sighed Minnie. "My picnic is over before it even started!"

Even the flowers that she had picked earlier looked glum.

Meanwhile, Donald was out walking when he saw Madeline standing near the blueberry bush.

"Welcome to the Clubhouse, Madeline!" said Donald.

"Thank you, Donald," replied Madeline. "Daisy and I were picking blueberries, but she went to get a bowl to put them in, and she hasn't come back."

"She could have put them in here," said Donald opening Minnie's basket. Inside he found his invitation to Madeline's surprise birthday picnic, and a shopping list.

Keeping Minnie's secret, Donald said "We'll see Daisy later, Madeline. Why don't you come to the grocery store with me? I'm going to make my special lemonade."

"I have a lemon tree at home in Overland Park. Bowen, Harper, Eleanor and I often make lemonade. It's my favorite drink," said Madeline.

Soon they arrived at the grocery store. Donald was so excited. He couldn't wait to make his special lemonade.

"Let me see," he said. "I need sugar, a jar of red cherries, six lemons and my secret ingredient—a lime."

While Madeline was getting the sugar and cherries, Donald went to find the lemons.

"Hmmm, they all look good, but that plump, juicy one at the bottom of the pile looks the best," thought Donald, as he carefully tried to pull it out.

"Look out!" shouted the shopkeeper. But it was too late. All the lemons tumbled onto the floor.

Donald picked up as many as he could before grabbing his parcel and racing out of the store, leaving Madeline and Minnie's basket behind.

When Donald got back to the Clubhouse, he looked in through the windows and saw Minnie and Daisy.

"My, they sure do look grumpy," quacked Donald. "My super-duper, secret-recipe lemonade is guaranteed to cheer them up."

Donald carefully cut the lemons and lime in half and squeezed them in the juicer. Then, he poured some sugar into a pitcher and added water, the juice and some ice cubes. Finally, he added a little cherry juice, and then slid a straw through each cherry for decoration.

"Hmmm, perfect for a picnic on a warm, sunny day!" said Donald after he tasted his lemonade.

"Madeline will love it!" he said with satisfaction. "Madeline, Madeline! Oh, no! I left her in the grocery store. I've lost our birthday girl! I've ruined everything!"

As it was such a beautiful day, Goofy and his kitten, Mr. Pettibone, were taking a walk in town. As they passed the grocery store, a lemon rolled out of the door. Mr. Pettibone pounced on it.

Goofy picked up the lemon and took it into the store. The storekeeper was picking up lemons that were scattered across the floor.

Goofy bent down to help, and spotted something on the floor by the counter.

It was Minnie's basket, and inside was an invitation addressed to him, and a shopping list. There was going to be a picnic, at noon, in the playground!

Just then, Madeline came over. "Hello, Goofy. Hello, Mr. Pettibone," she said. "Donald and I were buying ingredients to make lemonade, but he ran out when he knocked over all the lemons."

"Don't worry, Madeline, we'll see Donald later," replied Goofy. "We're going to the cornfield to pick corn for my special corn on the cob. You can come with us, if you like."

"I love corn on the cob!" exclaimed Madeline. "We always have it at picnics."

So, off they went, taking Minnie's basket with them.

Goofy

They walked down the road toward the cornfield. As they drew closer they saw rows and rows of stalks standing tall in the warm summer sun. Big, golden cobs hung heavily from the stalks.

"Just look at those huge ears!" exclaimed Goofy, licking his lips.

"Let's see, how many cobs do we need?" wondered Goofy aloud.

"Mickey will want one. Minnie will want one. That's two. I'm sure Donald will have two," said Goofy, counting up to four on his fingers. "Daisy will have one. Pluto doesn't eat corn, so we don't need to count him."

"I'll have five," said Goofy, "so that makes ten so far."

"How many would you like, Madeline?" asked Goofy.

"I'll have one, thank you Goofy. But they do look good. Perhaps we should pick a few more," replied Madeline.

Goofy gathered as many as he could carry, then called out to Madeline, "I'll take these to the Clubhouse, and then come back for the rest."

Madeline giggled as she watched Goofy sing and dance down the path leading to the Clubhouse.

Goofy was so excited! When he got back to the Clubhouse, he looked for the largest pot he could find and filled it with water. When the water boiled, he placed the corn in the pot, and added a pinch of salt.

Goofy forgot that he was supposed to go straight back to the cornfield!

Meanwhile, Mickey and Pluto were out enjoying a drive. Pluto loved to run, so Mickey stopped the car, and Pluto raced off into the cornfield.

"Mickey, Pluto. Am I glad to see you!" cried Madeline. "Goofy and I were picking corn, but we couldn't carry them all, so Goofy took some back to the Clubhouse. He said he'd come back, but I think he's forgotten."

"Don't worry, we'll give you a lift back to town, Madeline," said Mickey.

Just then Mickey spotted Minnie's basket.

"What's this doing here?" asked Mickey, lifting the lid. Inside he saw the invitations to the birthday picnic. "Come on everyone. We need to go to the grocery store before we head back to the Clubhouse!"

At the store, Mickey placed hot dogs, buns, ketchup and mustard onto the counter. "That's it!" he said, crossing off the remaining items on the shopping list.

Madeline looked over Mickey's shoulder and read the shopping list.

"That's strange," she said. "This morning Daisy and I picked blueberries to make a fruit salad. Then, Donald and I bought ingredients to make lemonade. Then, Goofy and I picked corn, and now, here we are, buying hot dogs, buns, ketchup and mustard!"

Mickey winked at Pluto. Then he noticed the clock on the wall.

"Golly! It's almost noon. We'd better hurry back to the Clubhouse," cried Mickey.

They grabbed their parcels, then ran out the door and raced back to the Clubhouse.

As Mickey, Madeline and Pluto drove toward the playground, they saw all their friends arriving, too.

"Oh, look!" cried Madeline excitedly. "There's Donald with his lemonade. And Daisy with her scrumptious fruit salad. Goofy can hardly see where he's going behind that pile of corn!"

Happy
Birthday
Madeline!

They stopped the car and greeted all their friends. Just then, they noticed Minnie sitting at a table all by herself.

She looked very glum.

"I hope we're not too late, Minnie!" cried Mickey.

"Oh, oh!" stuttered Minnie, surprised to see her friends. "I lost my basket with all the invitations in the garden this morning. So I thought Madeline's birthday picnic was ruined!"

"Birthday picnic!" exclaimed Madeline. "This is all for me?"

Minnie was so happy. She looked at the spread that her friends placed on the table.

"Fruit salad. Lemonade. Corn on the cob and hot dogs! Everything I'd planned for the picnic!" exclaimed Minnie.

Her friends had come to the rescue! They all laughed, and hugged each other and danced around in a circle.

"I found Madeline and your basket in the garden, so I thought I'd make a fruit salad. But then I forgot them by the blueberry bush," said Daisy.

"Well, I found them by the blueberry bush," said Donald. "I wanted to make lemonade. But then I left them at the grocery store. I'm sorry, Madeline."

"I bumped into Madeline at the grocery store," said Goofy. "We went to the cornfield. But I forgot them there."

"Pluto and I found them in the cornfield. I decided to get what was left on your shopping list," Mickey said. "I hope you're not angry with us?"

Minnie looked at her friends and the tasty spread on the table that they had provided.

"How could I be angry? You're the best friends in the world!" she said.

"You *are* the best friends in the world!" exclaimed Madeline. "Thank you for my surprise picnic, Minnie. And, thank you all for sharing my birthday."

"Happy birthday, Madeline!" they all sang together.

As the sun started going down, it was time for Madeline to return home to Overland Park where Bowen, Harper and Eleanor were waiting to celebrate her birthday as well.

In the meantime, everyone enjoyed Daisy's fruit salad, Donald's lemonade, Goofy's corn on the cob, and the wonderful hot dogs that Mickey prepared.

"This has been the best day ever!" Minnie declared.

"Hot dog!" agreed Mickey.

This personalized Disney Mickey Mouse Clubhouse book was especially created for Madeline Worster of Overland Park, with love from Mom and Dad.

0126 000000 0000 27 CC 0059